# little
# Miss
# Fickle

by Roger Hargreaves

PSS!
PRICE STERN SLOAN

Would you like me to tell you a story?

If you were Little Miss Fickle, you'd say, "Yes, please!" And then you'd say, "No, thank you!" And then you'd say, "Yes!" again.

Little Miss Fickle was one of those people who just could not make up their minds.

Ever!

About anything!

Little Miss Fickle lived in Dandelion Cottage which was on the outskirts of Sunnytown.

And she lived right next door to her best friend, Little Miss Neat, who lived in Twopin Cottage.

One Monday, Little Miss Fickle and Little Miss Neat went out to lunch in Sunnytown.

"I'll have the soup to start with," said Little Miss Neat to the waiter as she looked at the menu, "followed by the fish."

"So will I," said Little Miss Fickle.

But after the waiter had written down the order, Little Miss Fickle looked at the menu again.

"No, I won't," she said. "I'll have the salad instead, followed by the roast chicken!"

The waiter crossed out the first order, and wrote down the second.

"On the other hand," continued Little Miss Fickle, "I won't have anything to start with… but then I'll have the eggs!"

The waiter sighed.

An hour later, after the waiter had worn out three pencils and four order pads, Little Miss Fickle finally made up her mind to have the soup, followed by the fish.

The waiter brought the soup.

Little Miss Fickle looked at it. "I'm not hungry anymore," she said.

It was at that moment that the waiter decided he was going to be a bus driver instead of a waiter.

On Tuesday, Little Miss Fickle went to buy a hat.

"I want a new pink hat," she announced to the milliner.

The milliner brought her two pink hats to choose from.

"I'll have this one," said Little Miss Fickle, after she had tried them both on.

"Certainly, Madam," replied the milliner, and put the hat in a hatbox.

"On the other hand," said Little Miss Fickle, "I think I'll have the other hat!"

The milliner took the first hat out of the hatbox...and then she put the second hat into the hatbox!

"But," continued Little Miss Fickle, "I think the first hat suited me better, don't you?"

The milliner didn't say a word as she took the second hat out of the hatbox...and then put the first hat back into the hatbox!

She handed the hatbox to Little Miss Fickle.

Little Miss Fickle looked at the milliner.

"Do you have any blue hats?" she asked.

It was at that moment that the milliner decided she was going to be a ballerina instead of a milliner.

On Wednesday, Little Miss Fickle went to the butcher's.

"I'd like some sausages," she said.

"Beef sausages or pork sausages?" asked the butcher.

"Pork sausages," replied Little Miss Fickle.

The butcher wrapped up the pork sausages.

"But beef sausages would be nicer," said
Little Miss Fickle.

The butcher unwrapped the pork sausages, and
wrapped up some beef sausages instead.

"On the other hand," continued Little Miss Fickle,
"chops would be tastier!"

It was at that moment that the butcher decided he
needed a vacation.

But, on Thursday, guess what happened? Little Miss Fickle disappeared! Little Miss Neat had seen her pass Twopin Cottage on the way into Sunnytown, but she hadn't come back.

She didn't come back on Friday, either. So Little Miss Neat went looking for her.

She met Mr. Muddle. "Have you seen Little Miss Fickle?" she asked anxiously. Mr. Muddle looked at her in a puzzled sort of way. "Did you say, 'Have I been for a little tickle?' " he asked. "Oh, Mr. Muddle," said Little Miss Neat, and hurried on.

Then Little Miss Neat met Mr. Forgetful.

"Have you seen Little Miss Fickle?" she asked.
Mr. Forgetful thought.

"Well," she said, "have you?" Mr. Forgetful thought
again.

"Have I what?" he asked, after a while.

"Oh, Mr. Forgetful," said Little Miss Neat, and hurried
on.

But could she find Little Miss Fickle? No, she could
not! Nobody had seen her.

The Sunnytown Public Lending Library has…

nineteen thousand,

nine hundred,

and ninety-nine books.

On Saturday afternoon, Little Miss Fickle reached up and took one of them down from a shelf.

"I'll read this one," she thought to herself.

"On the other hand," she thought again, looking at another book, "perhaps I'll read that book instead!"

She put the first book back on the shelf, and took the other book down.

It was the nineteen thousand,

nine hundred,

and ninety-ninth book she had chosen!

Little Miss Fickle had been in the library for three days choosing a book.

Three whole days choosing just one single, solitary book!

She went home carrying her book.

That Saturday afternoon, Little Miss Neat was in the garden of Twopin Cottage when Little Miss Fickle walked past.

"Where have you BEEN?" she called out.

"To the library," replied Little Miss Fickle.

"For THREE days?" exclaimed Little Miss Neat.

"Well," explained Little Miss Fickle, "I wanted to choose the right book!"

And she held it up. And then she stopped and looked at it.

"Oh, botherations!" she said.

"I've read it before!"